THE SECRET OFFICE

Sara Cassidy

ILLUSTRATED BY
Alyssa Hutchings

orca Echoes

ORCA BOOK PUBLISHERS

For my sister Catherine, with whom
life is all joyous exploration. —S.C.

Text copyright © Sara Cassidy 2024
Illustrations copyright © Alyssa Hutchings 2024

Published in Canada and the United States in 2024 by Orca Book Publishers.
orcabook.com

Library and Archives Canada Cataloguing in Publication
Title: The secret office / Sara Cassidy ; illustrated by Alyssa Hutchings.
Names: Cassidy, Sara, author. | Hutchings, Alyssa, illustrator.
Series: Orca echoes.
Description: Series statement: Orca echoes
Identifiers: Canadiana (print) 20230544835 | Canadiana (ebook) 20230544843 |
ISBN 9781459839465 (softcover) |
ISBN 9781459839472 (PDF) | ISBN 9781459839489 (EPUB)
Subjects: LCGFT: Novels.
Classification: LCC PS8555.A7812 S42 2024 | DDC jC813/.54—dc23

Library of Congress Control Number: 2023946673

Summary: In this illustrated chapter book, twins Henry and Allie buy their mom a pair of headphones for her work-from-home meetings but soon discover something much better: an empty room in the basement that they can fix up just for her.

Orca Book Publishers is committed to reducing the consumption of nonrenewable resources in the production of our books. We make every effort to use materials that support a sustainable future.

Orca Book Publishers gratefully acknowledges the support for its publishing programs provided by the following agencies: the Government of Canada, the Canada Council for the Arts and the Province of British Columbia through the BC Arts Council and the Book Publishing Tax Credit.

Cover and interior artwork by Alyssa Hutchings.
Design by Troy Cunningham.
Edited by Sarah Howden.

Printed and bound in Canada.

27 26 25 24 • 1 2 3 4

1

"Jump!" Allie calls to Henry.

The two are running home from school in stormy weather, fall leaves swirling around them. Henry leaps, and the wind carries him for a full slab of sidewalk—he feels like a flying squirrel! When he touches down again, his heart is racing.

Allie and Henry reach the June Harriet Arms in record time and out of breath. They wipe their feet on all three of Mr. Jeff's welcome mats. Mr. Jeff, the new building superintendent, does not like dust, dirt or debris. As well as requiring people to wipe their feet three times before entering the building, he has put out a box with a sign that reads *If you've been to the beach, empty your pant cuffs into this box*. He has also hung a dog brush on a hook with a notice beside it: *Be sure to brush your canine before entering*.

Mr. Jeff is quiet, with lots of tattoos, and always has a paperback book tucked into his back pocket. When he isn't vacuuming, he is mopping. When he isn't mopping, he is raking.

"He's fastidious," the twins' mom, Sam, says. Henry found the word in the dictionary. It means "being careful that every detail is correct."

"He's too young to be married to a vacuum cleaner," their neighbor Makena says.

Allie leans close to the front door and slots the key on the string around her neck into the lock. She loves this moment of the day. Coming home! She and Henry have joked that their building is like a big hug, and that the sign maker made a mistake when they carved the words *June Harriet Arms* into the transom. It should be June Harriet's Arms. But who is June Harriet? They wonder about that a lot.

The twins pull the door open and enter the lobby. Mr. Jeff is on a rare break, his headphones off, reading his paperback in one of the lobby's plush red chairs.

"I love to read too," Allie says.

"I read to pass the time," Mr. Jeff answers, keeping his eyes on the page.

"You don't love books?" Allie asks.

Mr. Jeff thinks about this. "I don't think so," he says. "I loved a woman once, though."

"What was her name?" Allie asks.

"Allie."

"That's *my* name!"

Jeff looks at Allie and squints. "Well, you're not her. For one thing, she has red hair. Plus she is twenty years older than you."

"Henry and I are nine years old. Is she twenty-nine?" Allie says.

"Good math," Mr. Jeff says. "And I'm three years older than her."

Allie calculates. "Thirty-two."

"That's right," Mr. Jeff says.

"Do you miss her?" Henry asks. He can't imagine being apart from *his* Allie.

Mr. Jeff stares out the lobby window for a long time. Finally he stands and tucks his book into his pocket. He reaches for his vacuum cleaner, turns it on and starts vacuuming the hallway for the second time that day.

Allie and Henry push the elevator *Up* button. As soon as the elevator doors open, Allie yells, "Race!" She ducks into the stairwell while Henry jumps into the elevator and frantically pushes the button for the third floor and then the one that makes the doors close. As the old elevator shudders and heaves upward like an ancient rocket ship, Henry bends his knees and pumps his arms, preparing to run as soon as the doors open.

Ding! The elevator stops. Henry squeezes through the gap before the doors are fully parted. This is a great time-saver that he hasn't shared with Allie yet. As he sprints down the long hallway, Allie bursts out of the stairwell, just ahead of him. They fight for the lead, then crash into the apartment door at the same time, out of breath and each laughing that the other cheated.

As they tumble into their apartment, Sam scowls at them, finger on her lips. *Quiet*, she mouths. She is at her computer in the living room, on Zoom. It is clearly an important meeting. They can hear her director, Mr. Kahlil, going on in his squeaky voice about plans that need to be prepared and preparations that need to be planned.

Allie and Henry know all the people their mom works with, even though they have never met them. Ever since Sam started working from home, their voices fill the apartment. Some are high, some low, some quick, some slow. Some are warm, others seem angry.

Allie and Henry used to have the apartment to themselves after school (with check-ins from their neighbor Olive). They could watch TV, run the blender to make

anything-goes smoothies, build LEGO cities on the living room carpet—whatever they wanted. Now they can't do any of this. Instead they silently get their snacks from the kitchen, tiptoe to their bedroom, close the door tight and do their homework.

Today they get out their worksheets as soon as they close the door. It's Friday, and they want to get their homework done quickly so they can play all of Saturday and Sunday.

"Darn," Allie whispers, lifting her pencil from her math sheet. "I left my eraser at school."

Henry searches his pencil case. "Mine is gone. I used it all up, since I make so many mistakes."

"My teacher says that if you aren't making mistakes, you aren't learning anything," Allie says. She quietly opens the bedroom door. "I will have to brave it." She tiptoes into the living room. Then she gets down on her stomach and wriggles along the floor like a worm, out of view of the Zoom camera.

"Let's create a road map," Mr. Kahlil is saying, "of the strategic steps we'll take to reach our goal."

Allie wriggles to Sam's desk, then reaches up and blindly feels for the pencil jar. Sam shoots her a warning look. Allie lowers the cup and plucks out a rubbery white cube. Clutching it tightly, she slithers back to the bedroom.

"I'm so tired of Mom taking up the living room," she complains to Henry as she brushes dust off her shirt and pants. "I'm sick of crawling around and being quiet. I'm sick of Mr. Kahlil and his plans and strategies. I'm sick of the strange voices. It's like people have moved in, but they don't eat with us or help with the chores. It's like living with a bunch of ghosts."

"She needs headphones," Henry says. "Like Mr. Jeff wears to listen to music. Then we wouldn't have to hear everyone's voices."

"That's a great idea," Allie says.

For the next hour the two whisper together—not only to keep quiet but to plan a surprise.

2

Allie and Henry and Sam's apartment has one bedroom, a living room, a kitchen and a bathroom. Allie and Henry share the bedroom. Every four months they switch who gets the top bunk and who gets the bottom bunk. Whoever is on top has more privacy, but they have to climb down a ladder to go to the bathroom. And they can't have a bedside table. Sam screwed a hook into the ceiling and hung a basket so that whoever is in the top bunk can store their book and snack dishes before falling asleep.

The living room is Sam's bedroom and office. Every evening she removes the cushions from the couch and yanks on a handle, and her bed unfolds like a grasshopper. Every morning she turns the bed back into a couch. Then she opens her laptop on the coffee table to turn it into a desk.

The kitchen is cozy. The window looks out over the parking lot, but if someone stands on a kitchen chair, they can see across the town's rooftops, all the way to the sea.

Allie and Henry are making Toast Tray. It's a Saturday tradition that Sam started when they were six. They make a pot of coffee for her and cups of hot chocolate for themselves. They then toast nine slices of bread, three pieces for each of them. They load up the tray with anything they find that would be good on toast. Peanut butter, jam, honey, syrup, mustard, cheese,

mayonnaise, hummus, leftovers from last night's supper—anything. Then they have a toast party in the living room. They raise their steaming cups and propose toasts. "Here's to your excellent bedhead!" "Here's to the earwigs in the bathroom!" "Here's to a weekend without Zoom meetings!"

After this Saturday morning's Toast Tray, while Sam is in the shower, Allie and Henry search the apartment for coins. Allie plunges her hand into the depths of the scratchy armchair. She finds LEGO pieces, a plastic brontosaurus, a very short pencil and three dimes. When she reaches into the couch, she finds something exciting—an earring with a diamond. Meanwhile Henry fills his backpack with pop cans from the recycling box, which can be returned to the store for ten cents each.

As soon as Sam gets out of the shower, Allie shows her the earring. Sam picks her up and twirls her around. "That's from a pair that Grandma gave me. I thought it was lost forever!"

"I didn't know you had diamonds!" Allie says.

Sam shakes her head. "They're rhinestones. Cut glass. Not very valuable, but they reflect the light like a diamond."

"Do I get a reward?" Allie asks. "For finding it?"

Sam smiles. "How about a kiss?"

"I was thinking a dollar," Allie tries.

"What are you going to do with a dollar?"

"Add it to my allowance?"

"Right!" Sam snaps her fingers. "Allowance day."

Sam gets her wallet and gives the twins three dollars each, plus an extra dollar for Allie for finding the earring. Then, still in her robe, she starts cleaning up the kitchen. As she wipes the windowsill, she looks down at the building parking lot and murmurs, "I still can't believe we pay for that parking spot."

Allie and Henry laugh. "We know you can't!" says Allie.

Sam shrugs. "At least it's one less car."

Everyone in the building pays for a parking spot as part of their rent. But Sam and the twins don't have a car. Sam doesn't want one. Cars are bad for the environment, and the family gets around just fine walking and riding the bus. They use their old toy wagon for shopping or have their groceries delivered.

The twins don't mind. They've never had a car, so how could they miss having one?

They love riding the bus and dinging the bell when it's time to get off.

The twins put on their jackets and shoes, Henry moving slowly so the cans in his backpack don't jingle and give away their secret.

"Bye, Mom!" they call. "We're going to see Martha."

Martha works at the corner store where the twins often spend part of their allowance. She is also a jazz singer. Sam and the twins once went to one of her concerts, and she blew them a kiss from the stage!

"Left, right, left before you cross," Sam calls back. "And eye contact with the drivers. And enjoy the candy!"

Down in the lobby their new neighbor, Makena, is heading out for a walk with her poodle, Emerald. Emerald jumps up at Henry, yipping excitedly.

Makena laughs. "Emerald loves you so much, Henry. It's the cutest thing."

Henry doesn't think it's cute. He doesn't like Emerald's bad breath, he doesn't like getting his face licked, and he really doesn't like the sting of Emerald's claws on his legs.

"Did your mom tell you about supper tomorrow night at my place?" Makena asks the twins. "I'm making an eggplant casserole."

"Oh," says Allie. "That sounds nice." She has recently read a book about manners.

It takes some effort for Makena to get Emerald away from Henry and out the door.

Allie can tell that Henry isn't happy. "Don't worry," she says. "We can put ketchup on the eggplant casserole to drown out the taste."

But Henry isn't scared of eggplant casserole. He just wishes Makena's dog would leave him alone.

3

At the corner store, the twins cash in the empty cans for two dollars. With their allowances, the three dimes from the couch and the reward for the found earring, they have $9.30. They tell Martha about their mission to buy their mom headphones.

"Get her the kind that go over your ears like earmuffs," Martha advises. "They're comfortable." Martha suggests they try Chance Town, the thrift shop two doors down. "Be sure to test them before you pay for them."

Chance Town sells puzzles, coffee makers, armchairs, canoes, frying pans, computers, paintings of sunsets, video games, stuffed animals, tea towels, hand-made rugs from Iran and today an accordion with roses painted on it. Behind a set of glow-in-the-dark bowling pins, the twins find a pair of headphones. The clerk plugs them into the shop computer and starts a YouTube video of an orchestra playing Beethoven's fifth symphony. Allie plunks the headphones on her head.

"The sound is good!" Allie shouts over the music in her ears. "You try them, Henry!"

Henry gives his report *after* removing the headphones from his head. "They've got great padding. And I like that they're red. The trouble is, we're short $1.20."

Allie turns to the clerk. "Could you
lower the price?" she asks. "Please?" Sam
has taught the twins that *it never hurts to
ask*. But the clerk shakes their head and
says the price is "final." They also remind
the twins that there's tax on top of that.
Allie thinks, Ouch! It *can* hurt to ask!

"I have an idea," Henry tells Allie. "Let's look for more cans. There's got to be some around the mall."

Allie likes the idea. "We'll need"—she pauses to do the math—"twenty."

The clerk smiles and hands them a bag. "You can put them in here."

The twins tuck the headphones back behind the bowling pins and head outside. They immediately find eight pop cans in the flower beds in front of the grocery store. They use leaves to pick them up so their hands don't get sticky. They find four more cans in the garbage outside the fast-food restaurant, a few by the bench near the bakery and more in the tall grass above the river.

Finally they only need one more can. Allie spies it, an empty root-beer can in the roots of a riverbank tree. But as she reaches for it, her foot slips, and down

23

she slides, down the mucky riverbank into the cold river! Luckily the current is slow, and the river is shallow. Allie stands, knee-deep in the water, and raises the can in triumph. "Mom better like the headphones!" she yells.

At the store, Martha feels sorry for Allie in her wet jeans and soggy shoes. She pours hot chocolate into a paper cup and gives it to Allie for free. Allie shares it with Henry. *Slurp. Slurp.* The twins share everything. It's easier that way. Martha rings in the cans. They've got just the right amount.

The twins return to Chance Town and retrieve the headphones from behind the bowling pins. As they pay, they mention that the headphones are a gift. "Well, in that case," the clerk says, "let's give them some special treatment." The clerk removes the price tag, then wraps the headphones

in several layers of
purple and pink
tissue paper. They tie
up the parcel with
a pink ribbon, then
curl the ends of the
ribbon with a pair of
scissors. Then they cover the
gift with cat and dog stickers. "Ta-da!"

When the twins get back to the June
Harriet Arms, Mr. Jeff is polishing the
wide lobby mirror. As soon as he sees
Allie, he gets two plastic bags.

"Put these over those mucky shoes,"
he says. He eyes her dirty hands. "And
don't touch any walls on your way up.
Henry, you push the elevator buttons."

When the twins step into the apartment, they can't believe it. Sam is on a Zoom call. On a Saturday! Sam scribbles large letters on a piece of paper and holds it up for the twins to read. *Emergency meeting. Sorry!* It's Mr. Kahlil and a few other people from the office—Ellen, the funny one, and Pauline, who talks like a robot.

Allie gets changed, and then she and Henry crawl along the floor to Sam's desk. Sam's eyes light up when she sees their gift. Quietly, keeping her upper body still, she unties the ribbon and opens it up on her lap, out of view of the people in her Zoom meeting. She glances down and grins. She puts the headphones on right away and plugs them into the computer.

The living room goes silent. No more Mr. Kahlil's strategies and plans. No more Pauline's robot voice. Sam gives the twins a thumbs-up. Of course, when *she* talks in the meeting, the twins can hear her. And they still have to creep low, keeping out of sight. But it's better than it was before.

"Thank you!" Sam sings out as soon as the meeting ends. "These are comfortable. Great sound too. Everyone's voices were really clear."

"We like them too," Henry says.

"You've been so good, putting up with my noisy meetings." Sam takes the twins in her arms. "Did you use your entire allowance for these?"

They tell her how they returned cans to get coins to buy the headphones, and how Allie fell into the stream reaching for the last can. Sam opens her wallet and puts six quarters in Allie's hand.

"No," Allie says. "You don't have to pay us back. The headphones are a present."

"These coins are for the washing machine, to wash your clothes." Sam winks. "You can throw your runners in too."

The laundry room is in the echoey basement of the June Harriet Arms. The furnace is down there too, which makes the basement warm and dry. The ceilings and floors are painted a thick gray, and the walls are made of stone blocks. Allie always feels like she's in a castle when she's in the basement.

Mr. Jeff has put up a few signs in the laundry room. *Wipe down machine after use. Balance your load.*

Allie arranges her wet clothes and shoes evenly in the washing machine. As she pulls the quarters from her pocket, she knocks her elbow on the dryer, and the coins go flying. They clatter to the floor and roll in different directions. She scrambles on her knees and gathers them up—all but one. She searches everywhere for the last coin. Behind the washing machine. Nope. Under the dryer. Nope.

Allie finds herself in front of a door she has never noticed before. Where does it lead? She tries to peer through the keyhole, but it's gummed up with dirt. She puts her cheek to the floor and peers under the door.

"Wow!" she whispers. "What *is* this place?"

Sunday is Pancake Day. Allie and Henry are at the kitchen table, taking turns whipping the cream. It's a lot of work. Sam refuses to buy whipped cream in a spray can, because those cans are impossible to recycle. Instead she gets a carton of heavy cream, pours it into a bowl and hands the twins a whisk. They take turns, beating and beating until the cream thickens, then fluffs, then grows stiff enough to hold a peak like a snowy mountain.

"Stop!" Sam cries. "If you whip anymore, it will turn to butter!"

(The twins did once whip the cream too long, and the cream became a white lump in a puddle of thin water.)

Sam serves up the pancakes in stacks, with the biggest pancake on the bottom and the smallest ones—"silver dollars"— on top.

Usually the twins eat carefully, starting with the outer edges of the big pancakes. But today they gobble them down.

"You'll get stomachaches," Sam says. "What's the rush?"

"No rush," Allie says. She smiles at Henry.

Henry does not smile back. He hates to lie. Is keeping a secret the same as telling a lie? he wonders.

The day before, Allie found a screwdriver in the laundry room and used it to sweep her lost quarter from under the mysterious door. She got the washing machine running, then used the screwdriver to clean out the keyhole and get a better look. She saw a peaceful room— not big, but it wasn't tiny either. It was mostly empty, but Allie could make out some furniture in a stack.

She raced upstairs to tell Henry. He grabbed the periscope he got for Christmas. A periscope is like a telescope, but instead of letting a person see far away, it lets them see around corners. The trick is two small mirrors and two bends in the tube. Henry had been disappointed by the gift, but when he slid the periscope under the door of the locked room, he was very glad it was his.

What did he see? A room with stone walls, a table with two chairs stacked on top of it, and a rolled-up rug.

"The walls are dirty," he reported to Allie. "They're black! There's a window high on a wall, close to the ceiling. I wonder if we could find it from outside."

Allie clapped her hands together. "Good idea!"

The two ran outside and circled the entire building, peering into basement windows (and people's apartments!). Finally they found the secret room. They looked down onto the table and chairs and the rolled-up rug.

"It's so calm," Allie said.

"I wonder what's in the box," Henry said.

Allie frowned. "What box?"

"On the table. With the leather straps and the rusty lock." The box was the size of a laundry basket.

"Diamonds?" Allie wondered. The two laughed with excitement.

They talked about the mysterious room for the rest of the day and whispered about it when they were in their beds.

First thing Sunday morning, as soon as Henry woke up, he poked Allie awake. "I had a dream," he told her. "Someone gave us a key to the room. Guess who it was?"

Allie thought for a minute. "Mr. Jeff?"

"Yes!"

The two had decided to visit Mr. Jeff after breakfast. That was why they were wolfing down their pancakes now. They could hardly wait.

"We are invited to Makena's tonight," Sam tells them, pouring out glasses of orange juice.

"Yeah, she told us," Henry says quietly.

"Don't you want to go?" Sam asks him. "They have video games. And Emerald adores you."

Allie notices Henry bristle. "Is Emerald the problem?" she asks him.

Henry nods. "She licks me and follows me around and jumps in my lap as soon as I sit down. I understand that she likes me, but it's—"

"—oppressive," Sam says. "It gets in your way. It weighs on you."

"Yeah," Henry says. "I feel boxed in."

"Do you want me to talk to Makena about it?" Sam asks.

Henry shakes his head. "She will think I don't like Emerald."

"You could say you're allergic," Allie suggests.

"I'm allergic to lying," Henry says. "I can hardly breathe when I tell a lie. Lying is...*oppressive*."

"That's my boy," Sam says.

Sam and Henry both love words.

Sam puts a dollop of whipped cream on her pancake. She studies Henry's sad face. "Let me know if I can help, okay?"

5

When the twins are full of pancakes and have washed the dishes, they get their shoes on and tear downstairs—Allie in the elevator, Henry on the stairs. He runs so fast the handrail burns against the palm of his hand. It's an exciting feeling.

When the elevator slows down at the second floor, Allie's heart sinks. It's impossible to win the race to the lobby if the elevator stops on the way.

The doors shudder open. Their neighbor Olive, who has lived right below them all their lives, steps into the elevator with her cloud of white hair, a long black coat and boots with buttons up the sides. "Hello, Allie!" she says. "You look excited about something. I remember being young like you and filled with excitement—like a boat sail swollen with wind. But that was a long time ago. I just turned ninety-one years old."

Any chance Olive gets, she mentions her age. "If you add your age to mine, it adds up to a hundred years. This tiny moving room is carrying one hundred years!"

"I hope the ropes are strong," Allie says.

The two laugh.

"Most of my years have been happy ones," Olive says. "Light as sunshine. So we should be all right. I had a few sad years, but they were like stones dropped

into a pond. For some people, the sad years are just too sad to forget."

The elevator doors finally open onto the lobby. Henry has been waiting so long, he isn't even out of breath anymore from his run down the stairs.

"Henry!" Olive says. "I get to see you too? This really is my lucky day."

"I like your boots," Henry says.

"Thank you. Listen, you two," Olive says. "On Thursday morning, before school, could you help me carry a few boxes to the street? I have been doing fall cleaning. I didn't get around to spring cleaning! Chance Town says they'll pick up anything I leave outside."

"We'd be happy to," Allie says, remembering the rules in the manners book. "Right, Henry?"

"Yes," he says. "We're pretty strong."

"Wonderful! I'll see you Thursday morning, then." Olive heads toward the wall of gleaming brass mailboxes.

A vacuum cleaner revs up down the hallway. *V-R-O-O-M.*

"There he is," Henry says to Allie.

Allie takes a deep breath. "I'm excited."

"I'm scared," Henry says.

They watch Mr. Jeff vacuum for a while, Allie gathering her calm and Henry gathering his courage. As they approach, Allie notices a tattoo on Mr. Jeff's arm that she has never noticed before. It's a morning-glory vine curling around itself to spell *Allie*.

"Mr. Jeff!" Allie yells over the noise of the vacuum cleaner.

Mr. Jeff turns off the machine and looks into their faces. "What is it? Burned-out light bulb? Clogged toilet? Window that won't open?"

"No," Henry says. "Nothing like that."

Mr. Jeff's expression softens. "Having trouble making the rent?"

"No," Allie says. "Mom has a good job now. She works at home, actually. We have to be quiet and keep out of the way. It's really—"

"Oppressive," Henry says. "She works in the living room, so we can't watch TV or play Twister or build LEGO."

Mr. Jeff sighs. "There are no two-bedroom apartments available, if that's what you're asking."

"No," Henry says. "We aren't asking about that."

"We found a secret room!" Allie bursts out. She explains about doing laundry and the quarter rolling under the door.

"You found the coal room," Mr. Jeff says, leaning the vacuum cleaner against the wall. "Years ago, when they heated this building with coal, that room was where they stored the black stuff before it was burned. You'd go in there, get a bucketful and dump it into the furnace. If I was the building super back then, that would have been one of my jobs."

"We found the window and peeked in," Henry says.

"You did? A delivery truck would have backed up to that very window and emptied coal down a chute—which is like a metal slide—into the room. Then it would pull up the chute and drive on to the next building needing coal."

"Frosty the Snowman has two eyes made of coal," Allie says, remembering the song.

"Santa Claus sometimes leaves coal in stockings," Henry says. "But what actually is it?"

"It's a kind of rock, made out of plants that were squished together for millions of years."

"*Millions* of years?" Allie asks.

Mr. Jeff raises his eyebrows. "*Hundreds* of millions of years, actually. It burns nicely. It's very black."

"We really, really, really want to see inside that room," Allie says.

"Really, really," Henry adds.

"Really?" Mr. Jeff asks, smiling. "Well, I have been wanting to get in there and vacuum it out."

6

Allie and Henry hurry to the basement, hopping with excitement. But as they wait for Mr. Jeff to get his ring of keys, Henry grows quiet.

"What is it?" Allie asks.

"Makena's. I don't want to go."

Allie nods. "Because of the dog."

"Yeah." Henry stares at his feet.

"Are you sure you don't want Mom to say something to Makena? Or to Sonja and Ronaldo?" Those were Makena's kids.

"I'm scared they'll laugh at me," Henry answers.

Mr. Jeff comes around the corner, dragging his vacuum cleaner. "Who will laugh at you? You can't let anyone do that."

"Henry has a problem with someone's dog," Allie says.

"I know a bit about dogs. I used to work at a greyhound racecourse," Mr. Jeff says.

Allie frowns. "Making dogs race each other is mean."

"That's why I stopped working there. So what's the problem with this dog? Does it snarl or snap or something?"

"It's the opposite," Henry says.

Allie looks at Henry to check if she can tell Mr. Jeff more. Henry nods. "This dog is crazy about Henry," she says. "It follows him around and jumps on him."

"She trips me up and slobbers on me and even nips me with her teeth," Henry says.

Mr. Jeff sighs. "That's tough. You need to let the dog know you're bothered. You need to say 'down' or 'sit' when it's jumping up."

"I don't want to be mean to her," Henry says. His eyes are watery.

"How is that mean?" Mr. Jeff asks. "You're just telling that dog what you are comfortable with. Do it every time that dog bothers you. The dog will learn."

Allie eyes the door to the coal room. "Can we go in now?"

Mr. Jeff removes a key from the ring and hands it to her.

"It's heavy," Allie says. "Like a horse-shoe or that old bell Mom got at the thrift shop."

"Yes," Mr. Jeff agrees. "It's made of iron. These days most keys are made of steel."

Allie slips the key into the keyhole and turns. *Clunk!* The bolt slides out of the way. She turns the doorknob.

Allie and Henry step into the room and stare, awestruck. The room's walls are dark with coal dust. Light can barely eke through the dirty window, but the room is cozy and quiet.

"It's beautiful," Allie says.

"It's dry," Mr. Jeff says. "That's good. There's no outlet in here, though, to plug in my vacuum cleaner."

"Oh," Allie says.

"It's okay," he adds. "I'll run an extension cord in from the laundry room."

"Good!" Henry says.

Mr. Jeff looks at the twins with interest. "Why are you so interested in the electrical supply to this room?"

"Well," Allie starts, "because computers need to be plugged in."

"And lamps," Henry adds.

"Which are things," Allie continues, "that people need in..."

"...an office," Henry whispers.

Mr. Jeff wrinkles his nose. "Office? I don't understand."

"We thought Mom could use it for an office," Allie explains.

This was what Henry and she had been whispering about all night.

"I'm sorry, kids, but that isn't possible," Mr. Jeff says.

The twins' hearts sink.

"Why not?" Allie asks.

"This room isn't for rent."

"Couldn't we just use it?" Allie asks.

Mr. Jeff shakes his head. "The landlord would want you to pay."

"But it isn't being used," Henry says.

"Businesspeople don't think that way, I'm afraid."

Allie and Henry exchange a desperate look. "How about a trade?" Allie asks. "We could shovel the walks outside in winter. Or vacuum—"

Mr. Jeff reaches for his vacuum cleaner. "That's my job."

Allie wanders around the room. "It's got everything she would need. This table is big enough to hold her laptop." She lowers a chair from the table and sits. "This chair is sturdy."

Henry is staring at the big wooden box. "What is in there?"

"No idea." Mr. Jeff looks through the keys on his ring. "All these keys are too big for that lock." He gives the box a shake. "Sounds like papers."

"We get twenty-four dollars a month in allowance," Allie says. "Maybe that would be enough to rent the room."

"That would not be enough," Mr. Jeff says.

"We could add our Christmas money in December. We get twenty dollars each," Henry says.

"You kids don't give up, do you?"

"You have to ask for what you want," Allie says. "That's what Mom says."

Mr. Jeff looks at his phone. "There's a decent Wi-Fi signal. She would need that to do her work."

"So it's possible?" Allie asks.

"I will talk to the landlord. How about that? But on one condition." He holds up a finger. "Henry, you must tell Emerald to stop jumping up on you."

Henry's mouth drops open. "You knew it was Emerald?"

"Of course I did. I've seen what happens when she spies you in the lobby."

"Will she stop loving me if I tell her to stop jumping on me?"

"She will respect you," Mr. Jeff says firmly. "And respect is a form of love."

7

When they get to Makena's on Sunday evening, supper isn't ready. Makena explains that she forgot to turn on the oven. "I put the eggplant casserole in a while ago, but no good smells filled the apartment," she says. "I finally opened the oven door for a peek, and what did I see? A pale casserole on a cold oven rack."

Henry sticks close to Allie, hoping Emerald will mistake him for a shadow. But Emerald would never mistake him for anything other than wonderful Henry. Like any dog, she has a keen sense of smell.

Henry smells like chalk and cinnamon and fresh grass. Makena, Sonja and Ronaldo laugh as Emerald yips and jumps at him. But Allie and Sam watch with concern.

"Down," Henry says quietly to Emerald.

Emerald keeps jumping.

"Down," Henry repeats, louder.

Emerald jumps again but with less energy.

"*Down*," Henry says.

Emerald sits and looks up at him, her tail bashing against the floor.

Henry crouches and scratches her behind the ears. "Good girl."

Henry feels like a superhero. Like if he put his arms above his head, he would shoot up to the moon. Sam and Allie smile at each other, impressed.

Sonja and Ronaldo are a few years older than the twins. They always ask

Allie and Henry lots of questions about their favorite TV shows and what they're learning at school.

The twins help Sonja and Ronaldo set the table, and then they sit in the living room to play a board game called Clue. As soon as Henry joins the game, Emerald leaps into his lap. Henry takes her gently in his hands and puts her on the floor. Emerald leaps up again. Henry firmly puts her down again. Eventually Emerald curls up on the floor, her head on Henry's shoes. Henry doesn't mind that. It's actually quite nice.

The casserole takes longer to cook than Makena expected, so Sam suggests the kids head out to play soccer. On the way, Allie and Henry stop to say hi to Mr. Jeff, who is in the lobby plucking dead leaves from the plants. Henry tells him his

good news. "I did it! I told Emerald *down*, and it worked."

"I did something too," Mr. Jeff tells the twins. "I talked to the landlord about the room."

"What did he say?" Allie asks.

"He wants fifty dollars a month."

"We don't have fifty dollars," Henry says quietly.

"I talked him down from a hundred."

"Thank you," Allie squeaks. She's so disappointed, it's hard to talk.

The two join Sonja and Ronaldo outside for soccer. Henry plays goalie, using two hoodies on the ground as goal posts. He makes a few good saves, but then a shot zooms past him. He chases the ball into the parking lot. It rolls under a couple of cars and comes to rest in a dip in the parking space that his family rents but never uses.

"This silly spot," he mutters to himself. He looks up at the family's kitchen window and gives a little wave, though he's not quite sure who he's waving at. Maybe to himself the last time he looked out the kitchen window. Maybe to himself in the future. Maybe to their life in apartment 301, June Harriet Arms. We own this spot,

he thinks as he reaches for the ball. *We pay for it every month. And it just stands empty all day, like the coal room.* As he bends for the ball, it's as though a bolt of lightning zigs through him. He is electrified by a great idea.

Mr. Jeff listens carefully to Henry and Allie's idea. He pulls a notebook from his shirt pocket and thumbs through it. "There's actually a family moving in next week who asked if we had a second parking spot," he says. "According to your idea, you would rent your parking spot to them for fifty dollars a month, then use the fifty dollars to pay for the coal room."

"You mean, *Mom's office*!" Allie says, already celebrating.

But Henry is biting his lip. "There's a problem," he says. "Mom hates cars."

"Ohhh," Allie breathes out, like a balloon deflating.

"It's not a problem," Mr. Jeff says. He smiles. "This new family is looking for a spot to store their bikes and kayaks."

The twins stand by as Mr. Jeff taps numbers on his cell phone and then presents the plan to the landlord. After a moment he gives the twins a thumbs-up. The family's monthly payment for the parking spot will become rent for the coal room. The twins jump and hug each other.

8

On Monday Allie and Henry race home from school, wishing the wind was strong enough to make them fly. Mr. Jeff is waiting for them in the coal room with two buckets of hot, soapy water and sponges. The twins spend an hour scrubbing coal dust from the walls. As their sponges soak up the slick black powder, and the water in their buckets turns gray, the room grows less dark. They find a marvelous thing as they clean up the dust—an actual lump of coal. It's shiny and dark and shaped like a cube. It's very light.

Mr. Jeff grows quiet, looking at the piece of coal.

"You are deep in thought," Allie says. The *Book of Manners* says an observation is a polite way to ask how someone is feeling.

"I'm thinking about the older Allie," Mr. Jeff says. "She started a group that got her college to stop heating with coal. Burning it is bad for the climate and the air, and mining it damages animal habitat. Allie really cares about the world."

Mr. Jeff unrolls the rug. It is patterned with flowers. He revs up the vacuum cleaner, and each time he runs it across the rug, the reds and purples of the flowers become more vibrant.

"Petunias," Henry says when Mr. Jeff is finished. "Mom's favorite flower."

"It's like a magic wand," Allie says with awe. "That rug looked old and forgotten.

But your vacuum cleaner brought it back to life."

"The vacuum cleaner is a powerful machine," Mr. Jeff says, coiling the extension cord. Next he sprays vinegar on the room's one window and balls up a piece of newspaper. As he scrubs each pane clear of dust and dirt, daylight streams into the room and bounces off the white walls. "Cleaning is about letting light move."

After supper that evening, Allie and Henry work quietly, removing books and toys from a small bookcase in their room.

A shriek from the bathroom gets their attention. "The sink is black! And the towels! What were you two doing?" Sam yells.

After cleaning out the coal room, the twins had spent a while washing coal dust from behind their ears and the backs of their necks.

"Just playing in the dirt!" Allie answers. It isn't entirely a lie, she figures, since coal comes from the earth.

A few moments later, Sam calls out that she's taking the garbage down to the big bins in the basement.

"Okay!" the twins call back.

Here is their chance. As soon as Sam leaves, they write a note—*Gone to the Little Library*—then drag the bookcase out of the apartment. They slide it into a stairwell. It's a lot of work. They listen for Sam's return from the garbage room. As soon as they hear her go back into the apartment, they pull the bookcase down the hallway and into the elevator. They feel excited and sneaky at once.

They set up the bookcase in the coal room, add a few books and put the lump of coal on top, like a good-luck charm. On the way back to the apartment, Henry insists they stop at the Little Library, since they told Sam they were going there. That way they won't really have lied. The Little Library is a shelf near the lobby where people leave books they've read for others to pick up. Henry flips through a magazine about home decorating. He reads with interest an article about mirrors. It says that a mirror is a layer of glass laid on top of a layer of silver, and that a mirror can brighten up a room and make it feel bigger.

9

Olive is finishing her breakfast when the twins arrive on Thursday morning. "Breakfast is a very important meal," she tells them. "I would not have made it to ninety-one years old if I didn't eat a good breakfast. In fact, I would bet that I am half made out of oatmeal."

Olive shows the twins which boxes need to go to the curb. Allie and Henry nudge each other when they see a mirror sticking out of one of the boxes, alongside a lamp and a few plants.

"Could we have—" Allie starts to ask Olive.

"You can have anything you like," Olive says. "It's all getting donated anyway. I am happy to donate to you."

Outside, Ronaldo is returning from a walk with Emerald. Emerald leaps with excitement as soon as she smells Henry. As she rushes toward him, he kneels down and says calmly, "Hello, Emerald. Please sit." Emerald sits! "Good girl," Henry says.

After setting Olive's boxes at the curb, the twins take the mirror, lamp and plants, plus a kettle and two mugs, to the coal room. They position the mirror in line with the window so that it reflects light into the room. The plants make the room feel friendly.

"They'll keep Mom company," Henry says.

Mr. Jeff stops polishing the mailboxes the instant Allie and Henry enter the lobby after school. "I've been waiting for you," he tells them. He holds up a small key.

"Is that the key to the box?" Henry asks.

"I believe it is."

When they step into the coal room, Mr. Jeff whistles, impressed. "It's looking great in here! That mirror really helps the light move." He hands the small key to Henry. "You do the honors."

The key turns easily, and the lock springs open. Henry raises the box lid.

Inside the box are papers—newspaper articles, diagrams, photographs.

"Oh," Allie says. She was hoping for dollar bills.

"Interesting," Henry says, trying to be positive.

One black-and-white photograph shows a building halfway through construction. Another photo shows the building completed, with a small crowd in front of the entrance.

THE JUNE HARRIET ARMS

"It's the June Harriet Arms!" Allie says.

In the photograph, a woman with shiny short, curly hair is holding a pair of scissors high for the crowd to see.

"A ribbon-cutting ceremony," Mr. Jeff says. "To celebrate the opening of this building. That would be nearly a hundred years ago."

Allie studies a photograph of the woman with the shiny hair. On the back someone has written *Miss June Harriet, Architect.*

Henry gazes at it over her shoulder. "Did she build this building?" he wonders.

"She would have designed it," Mr. Jeff says. "She might have been the first woman architect in this city. And maybe the first Black architect! That's really something."

Henry unfolds several large sheets of paper. They look like mazes, but he and Allie soon figure out that they're June Harriet's floor plans for the building.

"Here's our apartment!"

"Here's the coal room!"

Mr. Jeff's cell phone buzzes. He reads a text and smiles. "Yesterday I asked the landlord for a raise," he tells the twins. "And he has just texted yes. I got it! Thanks to you two."

"Us?" Henry asks, confused.

"You two have taught me about asking for what you want. And working for it. In fact, today I texted an old friend that I had lost contact with, who I was missing very much."

"Did they text back?" Allie asks.

"No. But at least I tried."

10

"To the oatmeal that keeps Olive alive!"

"To the first—and dirtiest—of Mr. Jeff's three welcome mats!"

It's Toast Tray day. Saturday morning.

"To the big surprise we have for Mom!" Allie yells.

Sam looks confused. "Surprise? What surprise?"

Henry wipes his hands carefully on a napkin. He unfolds one of the floor plans, which Mr. Jeff let him borrow. "Behold the third floor of the June Harriet Arms."

"Amazing!" Sam says. Her eyes roam the page. "There's our apartment!"

Henry opens another floor plan. "This is the basement."

"Cool!" Sam says. "Where did you get these?"

"Can you find the laundry room?" Allie asks.

"And do you see a room next to the laundry room?" Henry asks. He tries to sound calm, but he is bursting with excitement.

"I do," Sam says slowly. "Is it a storage room?"

"Not exactly," Henry says.

"What is it?"

"Get your slippers on," Allie says.

"Grab your laptop," Henry adds.

"I get the feeling you are about to share a secret with me," Sam says, smiling. She pops a final bit of toast into her mouth.

"Yes," says Henry. "We're about to turn a secret into a *surprise*."

When they reach the laundry room, the twins ask Sam to close her eyes. While her eyes are closed, Allie turns the key and opens the door of the old coal room. Henry takes Sam's hand and leads her into the middle of the room.

"Surprise time!" Henry yells.

Sam opens her eyes. She takes in the desk, the bookcase, the petunia rug, the mirror and plants, the kettle and cups, the watering can the twins made from rinsing out a laundry-detergent bottle, the basket of tea bags and granola bars they squirreled from the kitchen, the extension cord snaking along the floor right up onto the desk. "What is this place?" she asks, astonished.

"Your office!"

Henry, Allie and Mr. Jeff are hanging a poster board on the wall beside the mailboxes. Mr. Jeff has devised a way to hang it without leaving marks on the wall. On the poster board are the photos of the June Harriet Arms under construction, the ribbon-cutting ceremony and the photo of June Harriet herself.

As soon as they get the poster board in place, Olive steps off the elevator to collect her mail. Her eyes light up as she studies the photographs. "June Harriet! My goodness." She points to a girl in the crowd at the ribbon-cutting ceremony. "There I am. And those are my parents beside me. We moved into our apartment the following week."

Tippity tippity tap. It's the familiar sound of Emerald's toenails as she trots across the lobby floor. But this time when Emerald sees her favorite person, she doesn't jump up or bark. She sits at his feet and looks up with watery eyes. Henry scratches her behind her ears and under her chin.

Mr. Jeff turns on his vacuum cleaner and gets to work. He doesn't notice the visitor at the front door, a woman his age, wearing a Lumber World shirt with a name tag that says *Allie*. She waves to the twins. They open the door.

"I'm looking for Jeff," the woman tells them.

"You mean Mr. Jeff? He's right there," Henry says, pointing.

"He is very good at vacuuming," Allie adds.

"Yes, he is," the older Allie says. "Some people believe we should each spend five minutes a day scrubbing some part of the world. Jeff does that and a lot more."

Grown-up Allie steps into the vacuum's path. Mr. Jeff looks up. He turns off the vacuum cleaner and lays down the hose.

"I got your text," the woman says. She opens her arms. "I miss you too."

The two hug for a long time.

The twins stare, smiling.

"Another surprise," Henry whispers to Allie.

KATRINA RAIN

SARA CASSIDY's children's books include finalists for the Governor General's Literary Award in Young People's Literature, Chocolate Lily Award, City of Victoria Children's Book Prize, Ruth and Sylvia Schwartz Children's Book Award, Diamond Willow Award, Silver Birch Express Award and Sunburst Award for Excellence in Canadian Literature of the Fantastic. Her book *Genius Jolene* won the Sheila A. Egoff Children's Literature Prize. She lives in Victoria, British Columbia, and works in communications for the BC Ministry of Health.

BRIAN LIMOYO

ALYSSA HUTCHINGS is an educator and illustrator based in Guelph, Ontario. She holds a BA in French studies and fine arts from the University of Waterloo and a bachelor of education from Queen's University. Her art style is whimsical and bright, and she strives to depict a sense of adventure in everyday life. When not making art, you can find her experimenting with vegan cooking and baking, sewing her own clothes, reading comics and manga, and playing board games with her husband.